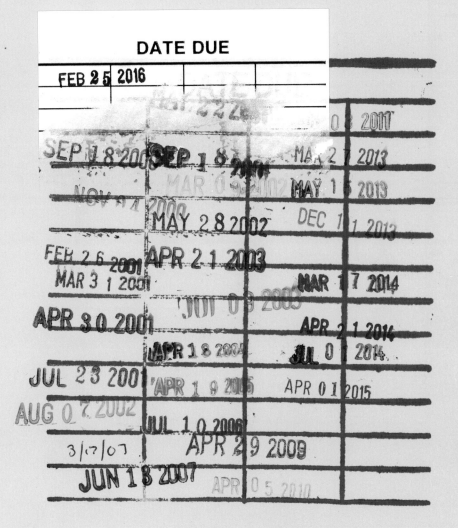

Mud Flat Spring

JAMES STEVENSON

Greenwillow Books · New York

For Gnomie,
spirit of spring

Watercolor paints and a black pen were used to prepare the full-color art.
The text type is Korinna.

Printed in Hong Kong by South China Printing Company (1988) Ltd.
First Edition 10 9 8 7 6 5 4 3 2 1

Library of Congress Cataloging-in-Publication Data
Stevenson, James, (date)
Mud Flat spring / by James Stevenson.
p.   cm.
Summary: The animals of Mud Flat celebrate
the coming of spring in their own ways.
ISBN 0-688-15772-6 (trade).
ISBN 0-688-15773-4 (lib. bdg.)
[1. Spring—Fiction.   2. Animals—Fiction.]
I. Title.   PZ7.S84748Mud   1999
[E]—dc21   98-2975   CIP   AC

Contents

·1·
Morgan

"Be very quiet," said Archie. "That's
Morgan's cave. He's hibernating,
and we don't want him to wake up."
"But spring is here," said Lois. "That's
when bears are supposed to wake up."

"I know," said Archie. "But when
Morgan wakes up, he is always
really grumpy. He makes everybody
miserable."
Just then they heard a growl from
inside the cave.
"Huh?" said Morgan, squinting.
"Do I hear birds? Is the winter over?"
He growled again.

"Morgan's waking up," said Archie.

"What should we do?"

Lois and Archie thought for a minute.

Then Lois said, "I have an idea."

She went to the door of the cave.

"Pardon me," she said.

Morgan growled. "What do *you* want?"
he said.

"I'm afraid I'm lost," said Lois.

"Could you tell me which way is south?"

"What do you want to know for?"
said Morgan.
"Ducks go south in the winter,"
said Lois. "And winter is coming,
and I am a duck."

"Winter is coming?" said Morgan.
"I thought it was almost over."
"No, no," said Lois. "Just starting."

"South is that way," said Morgan,
   pointing. He lay down and closed
   his eyes. "I'll just grab a few more
   months of shut-eye," he said,
   and went to sleep.

"How'd it go?" said Archie.
"Quite well," said Lois.

·2·
The First Crocus

"Look, children," said Mrs. Huff.
"The first crocus!"
"Nice flower," said Myrtle.
"It means spring is here at last,"
 said Mrs. Huff. "Every day it will
 grow a little bit more."

"It's growing a little bit right now,"
said Martin.
"It's growing a lot," said Myron.

The crocus was coming up
out of the ground.
There was a shower of dirt,
and the crocus fell over.

"Oops," said Bentley from under the crocus.
"Guess I wasn't looking where I was going."

"You have wrecked the first crocus,
   Bentley," said Mrs. Huff.
"I'll put it back," said Bentley.
"You can try," said Mrs. Huff.

 Bentley planted the crocus again.
"Good as new," he said.

"Let's hope so," said Mrs. Huff.
   She led her children away.

Bentley sat down by the crocus to rest.
Parker and Zooty came along.
"Hey!" said Parker. "The first crocus."

"I planted it myself," said Bentley.
"You did?" said Parker.
"Good work," said Zooty.
They walked down the path.
"Bentley has been down in the dark
    much too long," said Parker.
"He thinks he plants crocuses,"
    said Zooty.
"Spring will do Bentley a world
    of good," said Parker.

·3·
The Dance of Spring

Fergus was zigzagging around,
wobbling his head and
waving his feelers.
"What are you doing, Fergus?"
said Benjamin.

"I am doing a dance of spring,"
said Fergus. "Spring makes me happy,
so I'm celebrating."
"I want to do a dance of spring myself,"
said Benjamin.
"Go ahead," said Fergus.
Benjamin began to dance.

Just then Cheryl stuck her head
up out of the ground.
"What's going on?" said Cheryl.

"We are celebrating how warm
and nice it is," said Benjamin.
"We are doing a dance of spring,"
said Fergus.

"Is it hard to do?" said Cheryl.

"No," said Benjamin. "Just make up
  a dance and do it."

"Oh," said Cheryl. "I'm not sure
  I can do that."

  She stood up and waved and twisted.

"This isn't as hard as I thought,"
  she said.

Cheryl and Benjamin and Fergus
were dancing when Norton showed up.

"What's going on?" said Norton.

"The dance of spring," said Cheryl.

"Can I do it, too?" said Norton.

"Of course you can," said Benjamin.

Norton took off his cap and began dancing.

Then a bunch of others arrived
and joined in.

Douglas danced

and
Serena danced

and March

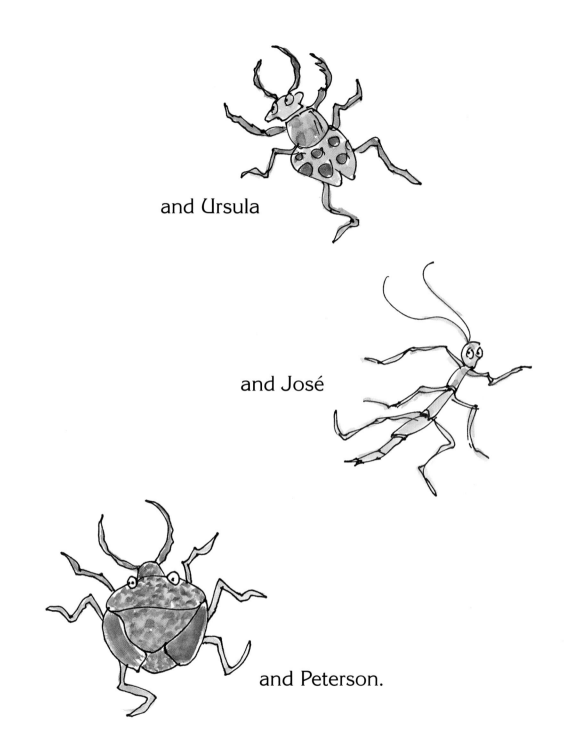

and Ursula

and José

and Peterson.

Then Albert came by.

"What's happening?" said Albert.

"We're celebrating spring," said Norton.

"Would you like to celebrate, too?"

"Oh, yes," said Albert.

"I love spring.

The warm sun,

the gentle breezes . . ."

Albert sat down
under a tree.
He closed his eyes
and gave a happy sigh.

"Aren't you going to celebrate
spring?" said Cheryl.

"You celebrate your way," said Albert,
"and I'll celebrate mine."
Albert began to snore.

·4·
Swamp

"Follow me, children," said Mrs. Sendly.

She led the way into the swamp.

"There is something you should all know."

"What could it be, Mama?" said Frank.

"Where are we going?" said Carole.

"There it is," she said. "The first
important sign of spring."

"It's a pretty green and red," said Carole.

"It smells good," said Frank.

"What's it called?" said Carole.

"Skunk cabbage," said Mrs. Sendly.

"*Skunk* cabbage?" said Frank.

"It's named after *us*," said Mrs. Sendly.

"And don't you forget it."

"Wow," said Carole.

"Cool," said Frank.

Mrs. Sendly led them back out
of the swamp.

·5·
Mr. Crocker
Goes Exploring

"Here comes that grouchy Mr. Crocker,"
 said Sid.
"It's hard to be nice to him,"
 said Tallulah.
"Let's try," said Ellen.

"Spring is here, Mr. Crocker," said Ellen.

"Hmph," said Mr. Crocker. "What makes
you think so?"

"The violets are blooming in the woods,"
said Tallulah. "There's forsythia, too."

"I'll believe it when I see it," said Mr. Crocker.

"The lilies of the valley are coming up near
the big rocks," said Ellen.

"So you say," said Mr. Crocker.

"I'd need proof."

He walked into the woods.

"Good-bye, Mr. Crocker," said Sid.

"Good-bye, Mr. Crocker," said Ellen.

"I told you so," said Tallulah.

Mr. Crocker hadn't gone very far
before he saw forsythia in bloom.
"Hmm," said Mr. Crocker.

He peered around a tree and saw violets.
"What do you know about that?" he said.

By the big rocks he saw lots and lots
of lilies of the valley.

"Well, well, well . . ." he said.

He picked a lily of the valley and
smelled it.

"The loveliest smell in the world,"
he said. "Oh, my, oh, my!"

Mr. Crocker moved through the woods.
"Primroses!" he said. "And hyacinths!
And bluebells, too!"

When Mr. Crocker came out of the woods,
Ellen and Sid and Tallulah were still there.
"You were correct," said Mr. Crocker.
"About spring?" said Tallulah.
Mr. Crocker nodded. "It's here," he said,
and went home.

·6·
The News

"Guess what?" said Barclay.

"What?" said Gracie.

"Tell us," said Rich.

"Spring is here," said Barclay.

"Here?" said Gracie.

"Where?" said Rich, looking around.

"Well, mostly up there," said Barclay, pointing.

"Oh," said Gracie. "Up where it's dry?"

"Yes," said Barclay. "That general area."

"We don't get up that way very much," said Rich.

"Well, it's worth a look," said Barclay.

"It only comes once a year." He swam away.

"Want to go up?" said Rich.

"Not especially," said Gracie.

"What is 'spring,' anyway?" said Rich.

"I have no idea," said Gracie. "I guess
  it's a turtle thing."

·7·
The Surprise

The evening was so nice, Watson could
hardly go to bed. He leaned out his window
and watched the sunset.

"This spring is better than any I remember,"
he said. "I hate to miss a minute of it."

The next morning Watson got a surprise.

Mud Flat was buried in snow.

"What in the world?" said Watson.

A few flakes drifted past his window.

"This certainly ruins spring
for everybody," said Frampton.

"Not necessarily," said Moira.

That afternoon
Roscoe and Willy
slid down Mud Flat Hill.

Moira and Daphne made a snow rabbit.

Everybody made tunnels in the snow.

Fred, Nell, Norman, Boris, and Sue
played rock hockey on Salt Pond.

"You know," said Norman. "I think this
spring is more fun than the last one."
"So do I," said Sue.

·8·
Just Checking

Morgan woke up again.

"It's got to be spring by now," he said.

"I bet those kids were just trying to trick me."

He got up and lumbered to the door
of his cave.
There was snow everywhere.
"Still winter," said Morgan, and went
back to sleep.

·9·
Two for One

"Some weird weather," said Malcolm.

"Just when we were having a lovely spring."

"On the other hand," said Burford,

"when this snow melts, we'll have spring
 all over again."

"I hadn't thought of that," said Malcolm.

"We're very lucky this year,"
 said Burford. "Two springs."

"I can't wait for the next one," said Malcolm.